JUST A PIGGY BANK

BY GINA AND MERCER MAYER

How true it is!

*For
Zeb, Baby Ben,
Arden, Jessie, and
Big Ben*

A GOLDEN BOOK • NEW YORK

Golden Books Publishing Company, Inc., New York, New York 10106

Just a Piggy Bank book, characters, text, and images © 2001 Gina and Mercer Mayer. LITTLE CRITTER, MERCER MAYER'S LITTLE CRITTER, and MERCER MAYER'S LITTLE CRITTER Logo are registered trademarks of Orchard House Licensing Company. All rights reserved. Printed in the U.S.A. No part of this book may be reproduced or copied in any form without written permission from the copyright owner. GOLDEN BOOKS®, A GOLDEN BOOK®, G DESIGN®, and the distinctive spine are registered trademarks of Golden Books Publishing Company, Inc. A GOLDEN STORYBOOK™ is a trademark of Golden Books Publishing Company, Inc. Library of Congress Catalog Card Number: 2001086775   ISBN: 0-307-13283-8   First Edition 2001
10 9 8 7 6 5 4 3 2 1

Grandpa gave me a piggy bank so I could save my money. He gave one to my little sister, too.

But I didn't have any money. So Grandma
gave me some.

Grandma gave my little sister some money, too. My little sister put her money in her piggy bank and took it upstairs to her room.

I put my money in my pocket. I'll put it in my piggy bank later.

Just then, my friends came by. They were going to the corner store. I decided to go with them since I had money.

First I picked out some candy.

Then I got some gum.

I also bought a soda.

When I got home, I wanted to put the rest of
my money in my piggy bank. But all I had left
were three pennies!

"Mom!" I said. "I don't have any money to put in my piggy bank. I need some."

Mom said I could clean up the mess in the living room to earn some money. I was too tired so I went outside to play with my puppy.

Later, I asked Mom for my money.
She said, "What did you do for it?"
I said, "I played with my puppy." Mom
didn't think I deserved money for that.

So I cleaned up the mess in the living room. Mostly it wasn't even my mess. Then Mom gave me some money.

"Now put it in your piggy bank for safekeeping," she said.

I said I would, but first I needed to play my video game.

I forgot all about my money until bedtime. I couldn't find it anywhere. I didn't have a good night.

A few days later, Mom took me and my little sister to the grocery store. My little sister got to buy a pack of trading cards because she had her own money.

I asked Mom if I could get a pack of trading cards,
too. Mom asked me if I brought my own money.
  "I lost it!" I cried.

Mom said she would buy the cards for me. But I would have to do a bunch of chores when I got home.

First I had to put all of my dirty clothes in the hamper.

Then I had to empty the dishwasher . . .

and sweep the kitchen.

Finally, Mom said that I had earned my trading cards. But I still didn't have any money to put in my piggy bank.

"Well," said Mom, "to earn more money, you'll have to do more chores."

CHORES
☐ Feed cat
☐ Put away books
☐ Pick up toys
☐ Bikes on porch

So I put all of the books
back on the bookshelf . . .

and brought in all of
the toys from the yard.

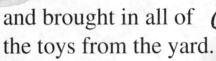

I even put my bicycle
on the porch.

Then Mom gave me money.

I ran right upstairs and
put it in my piggy bank.

Mom says that I can earn money every week
if I do extra chores. I don't know about that.
It is just getting too hard to be a kid!